HAPPY BLANKET

Tony Ross

Farrar, Straus and Giroux
New York

Gregory had a blanket that made him feel happy.

He called it his Happy Blanket.

Although Gregory wasn't afraid of the dark,

he was even less afraid of it when he had his Happy Blanket.

"You shouldn't go out with that yucky old rag!

It makes you look silly," said awful Aunt Maggie.

"It isn't a yucky old rag," said Gregory. "It's a spaceship."

And he zoomed out to play in the stars.

"You shouldn't put that dirty old thing in your mouth.

It's bad for you and your nose may fall off," said Grandpa.

"It's not a dirty old thing!" said Gregory. "It's a pirate ship."

And he sailed south to the Spanish Main.

"Don't you think you are a bit old for a gooey old blanket?

Only babies have those," said Uncle Sid.

"It's not a gooey old blanket. It's a suit of armor,"

said Gregory, waving his sword at a dragon.

When the dragon was dead,

Gregory went for a walk in the park.

Suddenly, around a corner, he heard a horrible noise.

"Wooooooooohh!" it went. "Yeeeeeeeeerr!" went Gregory.

"It must be something terrible,"

I'd better be off ...

cried Gregory. "Yeeeeeeeerr! HELP!

… on my magic carpet."

And the magic carpet saved him from the claws of a big growly bear.

The End.

The End.

And the bear chased away a magician on a flying carpet.

cried Lucy. "Wooooooooohh! HELP!"

went her big growly bear.

"It must be something dreadful,"

"Grrrrrrrrr! Grrrrrrrrr!"

Suddenly, she thought she heard a strange noise from around a corner.

"Wooooooooohh!" went Lucy. "Yeeeeeeeeerr!" it went.

So Lucy took her big growly bear to the park,

where nobody would put him into the washing machine.

"No!" said Lucy.

"It's the big growly bear who looks after me."

Once, Mom tried to take her blanket away.

"It's ready for the wash!" she said.

But Lucy took it back again.

"It's the big growly bear who looks after me," she said.

Once, Dad took her blanket away

and threw it in the garbage. ("Dirty old thing," he said.)

Her Happy Blanket looked after her all the time,

even when she was asleep.

Then, one day, Lucy found a Happy Blanket,

and she felt safe.

… **dark shadows and things on TV**

… **that she just *had* to watch.**

Lucy was afraid of nearly everything.

Spiders in the bath . . .

HAPPY BLANKET

Tony Ross

Farrar, Straus and Giroux
New York